A Christmas Story for HAYLEY

By Suzanne Marshall

LiveWellMedia.com

ISBN-13: 978-1976024467
ISBN-10: 1976024463

This book is
dedicated to:

HAYLEY

who is loved
very much!

At Christmastime this year,
a humbug mood fills the air,
and signs of Christmas disappear.

But never fear,
Hayley is here!

Yes, that's YOU.
Here's what you do...

☀ HAYLEY ☀

with a set of pencils and pens,
you draw signs of Christmas again.
First, a sketch of a snowy friend...

And when the sketch
is clear to see,
a squirrel twirls happily.

❄ HAYLEY ❄
next you sketch a tree and star,
spreading peace near and far.

And when the sketch
is clear to see,
a bear grins gratefully.

When you draw ornaments
HAYLEY
for fun and festivity...

...a mouse
squeaks
merrily.

HAYLEY

when you sketch a Christmas wreath,
spreading kindness and goodwill...

...a friendly fox
is truly thrilled.

HAYLEY

when you sketch a Christmas stocking,
a bunny rabbit starts a' hopping.

HAYLEY

when you sketch some bells for ringing
to spread the joy of love and giving...

...a cheerful birdie
starts a' singing.

HAYLEY

when you sketch three Christmas candles,
spreading light, blissful and bright...

...a penguin giggles
with delight.

HAYLEY

when you draw a Christmas dove,
everyone feels a bounty of love.

HAYLEY

when you sketch a sweet Reindeer,
Santa gives three jolly cheers.

Christmas spirit
is truly here!

HAYLEY

next you sketch three gifts with bows
even though you already know:
the greatest gift has no box or card;
the greatest gift is in your heart.

HAYLEY

because you dared, because you cared,
you saved the spirit of Christmas this year!

You are loved, Hayley,
every day of the year!

Merry Christmas

HAYLEY

Coloring Pages Instructions

* Use crayons or colored pencils (not markers).

* Color inside, outside, through the lines, wherever you want!

* Make your own rules because this is *your* book.

Special Thanks

to Mom and Dad as well as my awesome editorial team: Rachel and Hannah Roeder, and Don Marshall. Illustrations have been edited by the author. Polar bear, penguin, lantern: © dazdraperma at fotosearch.com. Bear, fox, mouse, reindeer, squirrel, bells, gifts, tree, wreath: © InhaSemiankova at fotosearch.com. Bird: © hermandesign2015 at fotosearch.com. Candles: © antimartina at fotosearch.com. Background elements, angel, bunny, santa, additional sketches from freepik.com.

About the Author

An honors graduate of Smith College, Suzanne Marshall writes to inspire, engage and empower children. View more of her personalized children's books at: **LiveWellMedia.com**.

Made in the USA
Monee, IL
09 December 2021

84513283R00026